The Three Little Pigs

Retold by **Bonnie Dobkin**

Illustrated by **Subash Bajaj**

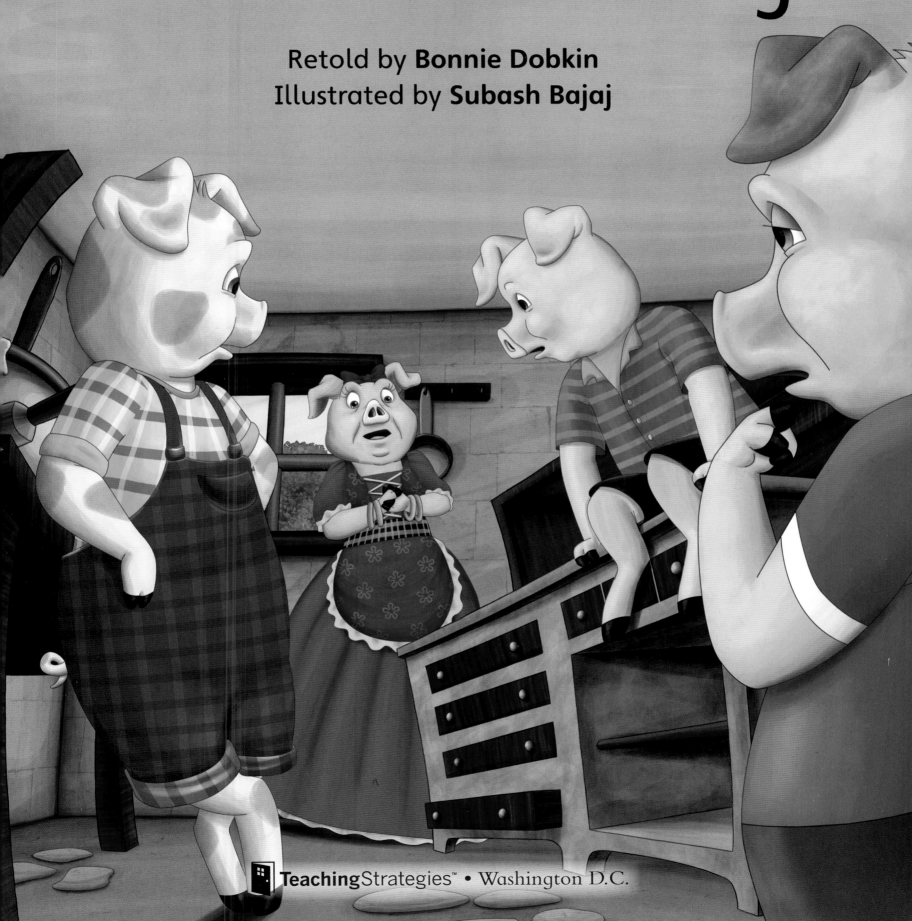

TeachingStrategies™ • Washington D.C.

For Teaching Strategies, Inc.
Publisher: Larry Bram
Editorial Director: Hilary Parrish Nelson
VP Curriculum and Assessment: Cate Heroman
Product Manager: Kai-leé Berke
Book Development Team: Sherrie Rudick and Jan Greenberg
Project Manager: Jo A. Wilson

For Q2AMedia
Editorial Director: Bonnie Dobkin
Editor and Curriculum Adviser: Suzanne Barchers
Program Manager: Gayatri Singh
Creative Director: Simmi Sikka
Project Manager: Santosh Vasudevan
Illustrator: Subash Bajaj
Designer: Ritu Chopra

Teaching Strategies, Inc.
P.O. Box 42243
Washington, DC 20015
www.TeachingStrategies.com

ISBN: 978-1-60617-135-6

Library of Congress Cataloging-in-Publication Data
Dobkin, Bonnie.
  The three little pigs / retold by Bonnie Dobkin ; illustrated by Subash Bajaj.
      p. cm.
  Summary: Relates the adventures of three little pigs who leave home to seek their fortunes
  and how they deal with the big bad wolf.
  ISBN 978-1-60617-135-6
  [1. Folklore. 2. Pigs--Folklore.] I. Bajaj, Subash, ill. II. Three little pigs. English. III. Title.
  PZ8.1.D674Th 2010
  398.24'529633--dc22
                                    2009044303

CPSIA tracking label information:
RR Donnelley, Shenzhen, China
Date of Production: February 2011
Cohort: Batch 2

Printed and bound in China

2 3 4 5 6 7 8 9 10	15 14 13 12 11
Printing	Year Printed

Once upon a time, three little piglets lived in a small, cozy home with their mother. Their names were Porter, Perry, and Parker.

Porter was a relaxed sort of pig.
He liked to play, eat, and sleep.

Perry was a creative type of pig.
He had lots of ideas, but he didn't
always finish what he started.

And Parker was a thoughtful little pig who worked hard and did everything just the way he was supposed to.

This kind of annoyed his two brothers.

5

Well, the three little piglets got older and older, and bigger and rounder. One day their mother made a decision.

"You've grown too big for this little house," she said. "It's time for you all to go off into the wide, wide world and build homes of your own."

So the three pigs packed their bags and got ready to leave their too-cozy home.

"Any advice for us, Mother?" asked Parker.

"Why, yes," said their mother. "Watch out for that no-good big bad wolf who's always skulking around."

"And remember . . .

Always work hard; remember to plan.
And whatever you do,
do the best that you can."

8

The three pigs kissed their mother
good-bye. Then they trotted out
of the house, down the road,
and out of the village.

Before they had gone very far, they came to a big field full of golden haystacks.

"You know," said Porter quickly, "I think I'll build my house of straw. It's a nice color. And the house will be easy to build!"

"I'm not sure this is a good plan," said Parker. "Will it be warm enough? Will it keep out the rain? What will happen when the wind is strong?"

Porter rolled his eyes. "It will be a great house," he said. "And I'll still have time to play when I'm done."

"Then good luck to you!" said Perry and Parker. And they continued down the road.

Soon Parker and Perry came
to a shady grove of trees.

"You know," said Perry, "I think I'll build
my house of logs. Logs are strong, and
I can paint them different colors."

"That sounds like a good plan," said
Parker, "if you finish what you start."

"I will," said Perry. And he waved
as Parker continued down the road.

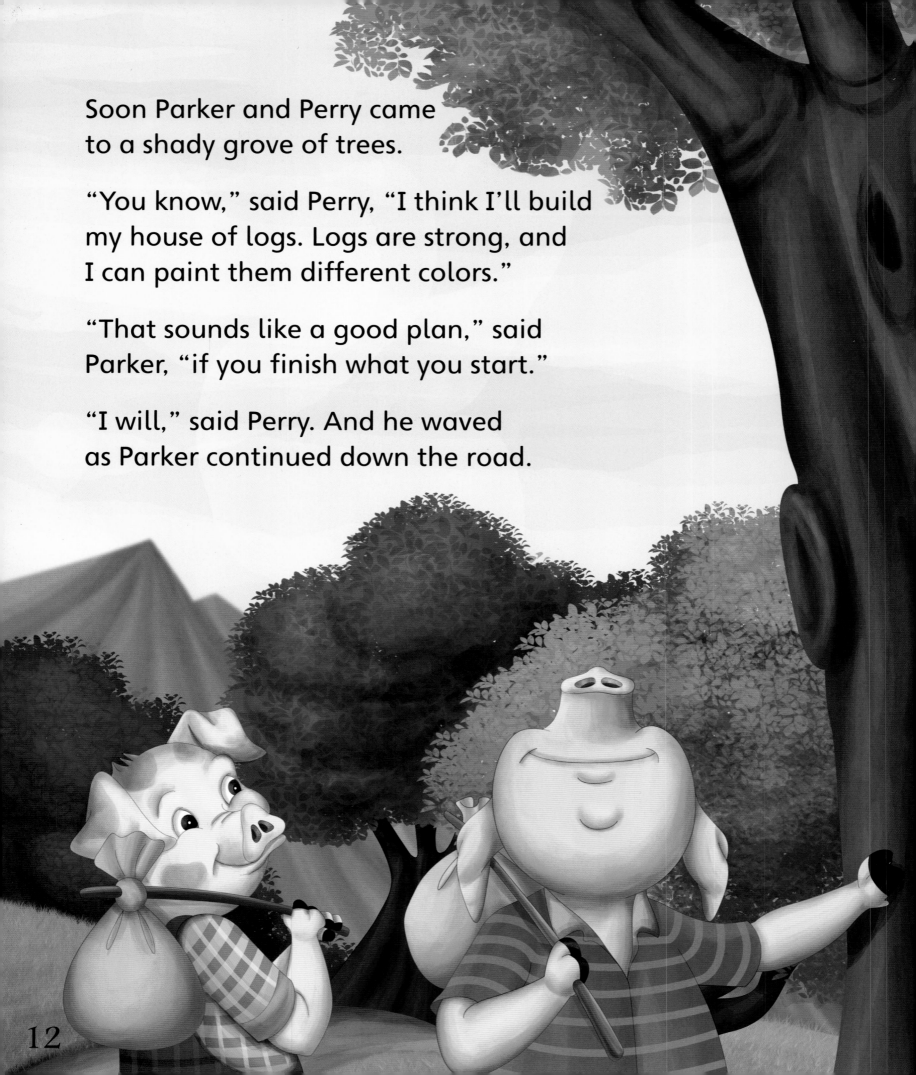

Perry stood and looked up at the trees.

"Hmmm," he said. "Cutting down those trees would take a long time. I'll just build my house from the sticks on the ground instead."

And that's exactly what he did!

Further down the road, Parker was busily planning his house. He bought bricks and stone and mortar for the walls. He bought strong oak planks for the doors.

He worked on the house for days and days. But when he was done, he felt happy.

"Mother would be proud," he said. "I worked hard, and I made my house the best it could be."

Now, what none of the pigs realized was that someone very bad knew that they had left their mother's house.

And who do you think that someone was?
Yes! It was the no-good big bad wolf.

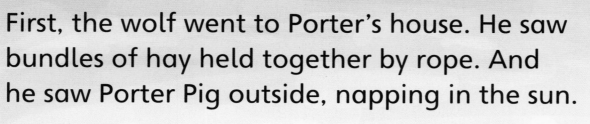

First, the wolf went to Porter's house. He saw bundles of hay held together by rope. And he saw Porter Pig outside, napping in the sun.

"Hello, pig," said the wolf.

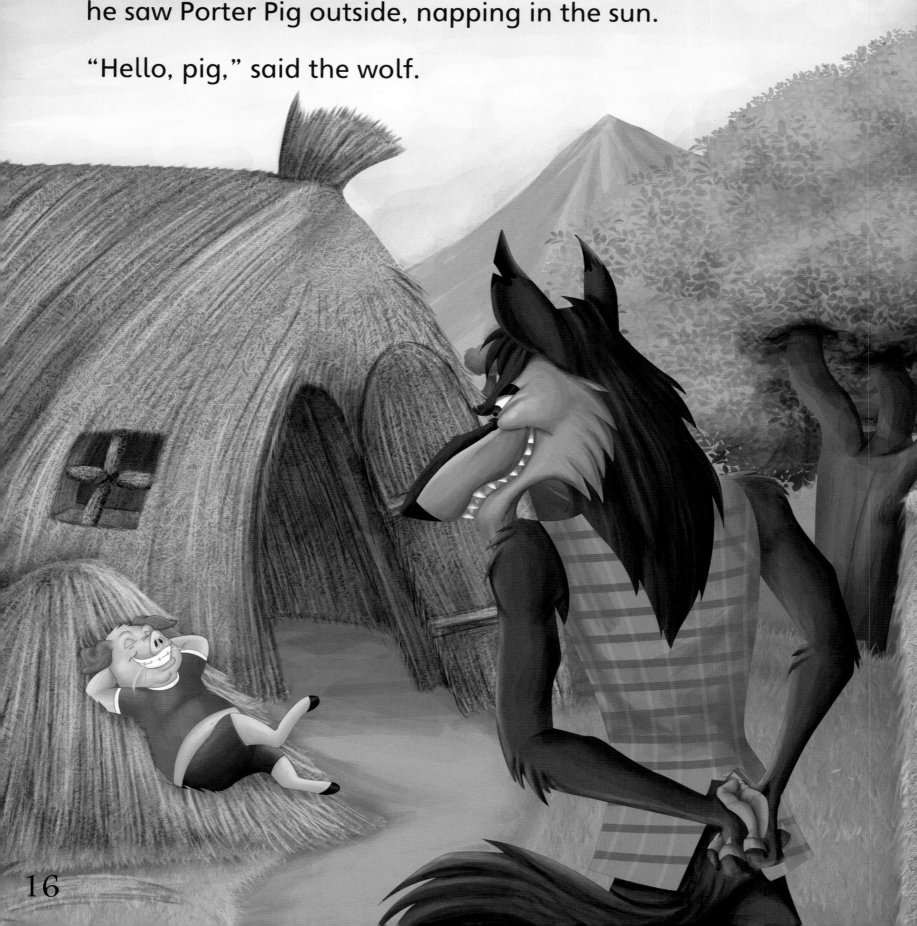

Porter opened his eyes, squealed, and jumped
to his feet. He ran into his house, pushed the
door shut, and hid under his bed.

"Now, now," said the wolf. I only want to have a chat."

"Ha!" said Porter. "I know a hungry wolf when I see one!"

"It really doesn't matter," said the wolf.
"*Little pig, little pig, let me come in.*"

"Are you kidding?" said Porter.
"*Not by the hair of my chinny-chin-chin!*"

"*Then I'll huff, and I'll puff, and I'll BLOW your house in!*"

18

The wolf stepped back. Then he huffed.
And he puffed. And he BLE-E-E-EW with all his might!

The straw house flew apart!
The wolf pounced.
The pig bounced.
But Porter squealed and ran!

"Hmmm," said the wolf. "Unfortunate."

The next day, the wolf decided to try again. He strolled down the road until he saw a flimsy house made of sticks and twigs. Perry was lying in a hammock outside.

"Hello, my little piggy" said the wolf.

Perry jumped up in fright. He ran inside his shaky house and pushed a dresser against the door.

"Hah," said the wolf.
"Does he really think that's going to help?"
He cleared his throat.

"Little pig, little pig, let me come in."

"No way!" said Perry. *"Not by the hair of my chinny-chin-chin!"*

"Then I'll huff, and I'll puff, and I'll BLOW your house in!"

The wolf stepped back. He took two huffs.
And he took two puffs. And then he BLE-E-E-EW
with all his might!

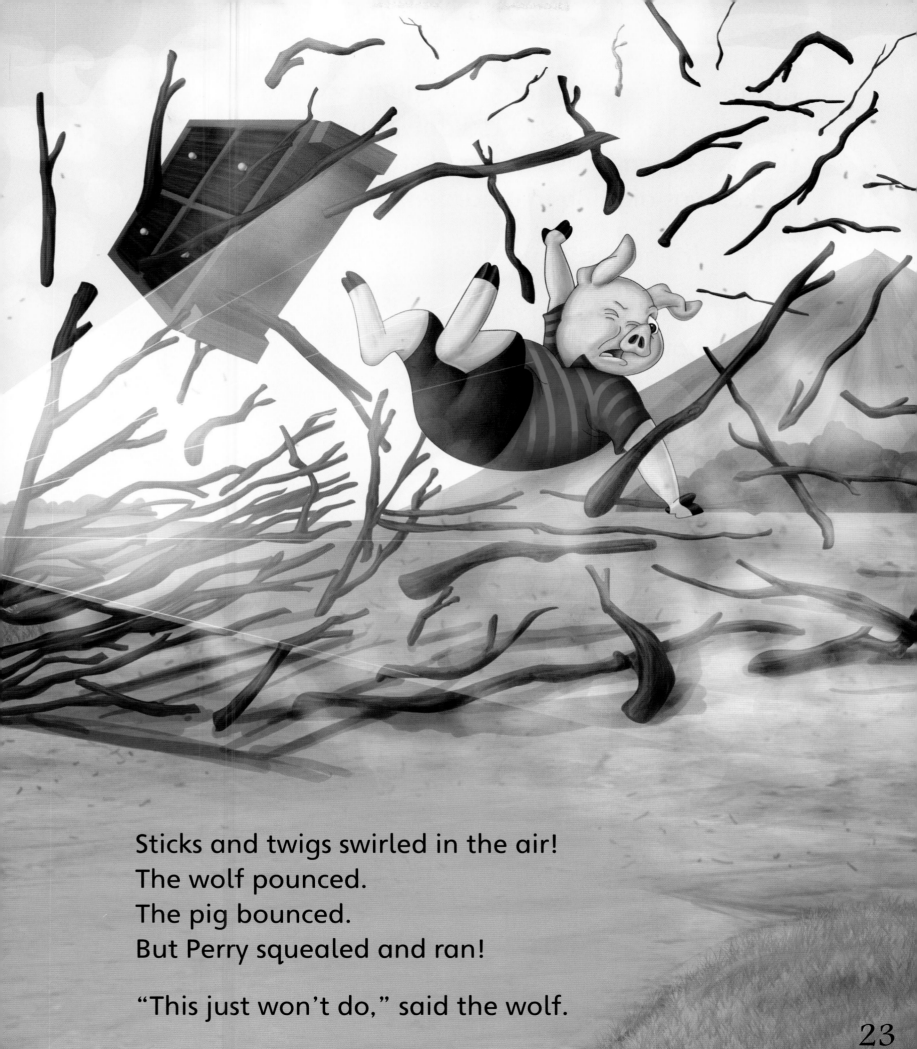

Sticks and twigs swirled in the air!
The wolf pounced.
The pig bounced.
But Perry squealed and ran!

"This just won't do," said the wolf.

But the wolf knew there was still one more brother to visit. He strolled down the road until he saw a house made of stone and brick. Parker was digging in a garden outside.

"Hello, friend pig" said the wolf.

"Don't you friend pig me," said Parker. "Leave now, or you'll be sorry!"

"I doubt it." said the wolf.

Parker went inside and slammed the door. The wolf heard three locks locking and four shutters slamming. He stood back.

"Little pig, little pig, let me come in!"

"Not by the hair of my chinny-chin-chin!"

"Then I'll huff, and I'll puff, and I'll BLOW your house in!"

"Go ahead and try!" said Parker.

The wolf huffed three times. He puffed
three times. And then he BLE-E-E-EW
with all his might.

Nothing happened.

"That's a surprise," said the wolf.

26

Now he huffed four times. And he puffed four times. And them he BLE-E-E-EW again with all his might.

Still nothing. The wolf tried again. And again. And again.

"This is not going at all the way I expected," he said.

Finally, the wolf fell flat on his back, puffing and wheezing.

He heard the shutter creak open.

"I knew my house would stand up to that no-good wolf," said Parker. "I'm just glad he didn't think about coming down the chimney!"

The shutter slammed shut.

"The chimney!" whispered the wolf, springing to his feet. "Of course!"

He sneaked to the side of the house and saw pile of boxes stacked against the wall.

"This makes it even easier," he chuckled. He climbed up the boxes. He crept across the roof. Then he jumped into the opening and slid down the chimney!

But down below, water bubbled in a big black kettle that was hanging in the fireplace. Parker threw more wood onto the roaring fire.

"Here I come, little pig!" said the wolf. "You weren't so clever after all!"

"Oh, no?" said Parker.

The wolf landed in the kettle with a loud *kerplunk!*
Water steamed and boiled around him. The wolf
ho-o-o-owled in pain and shot right back up the chimney!

The water had boiled off half his fur!

"Oh, no!" cried the wolf. He was so embarrassed that he left the country, never to be seen again.

Porter and Perry moved in with their brother and they lived happily ever after.